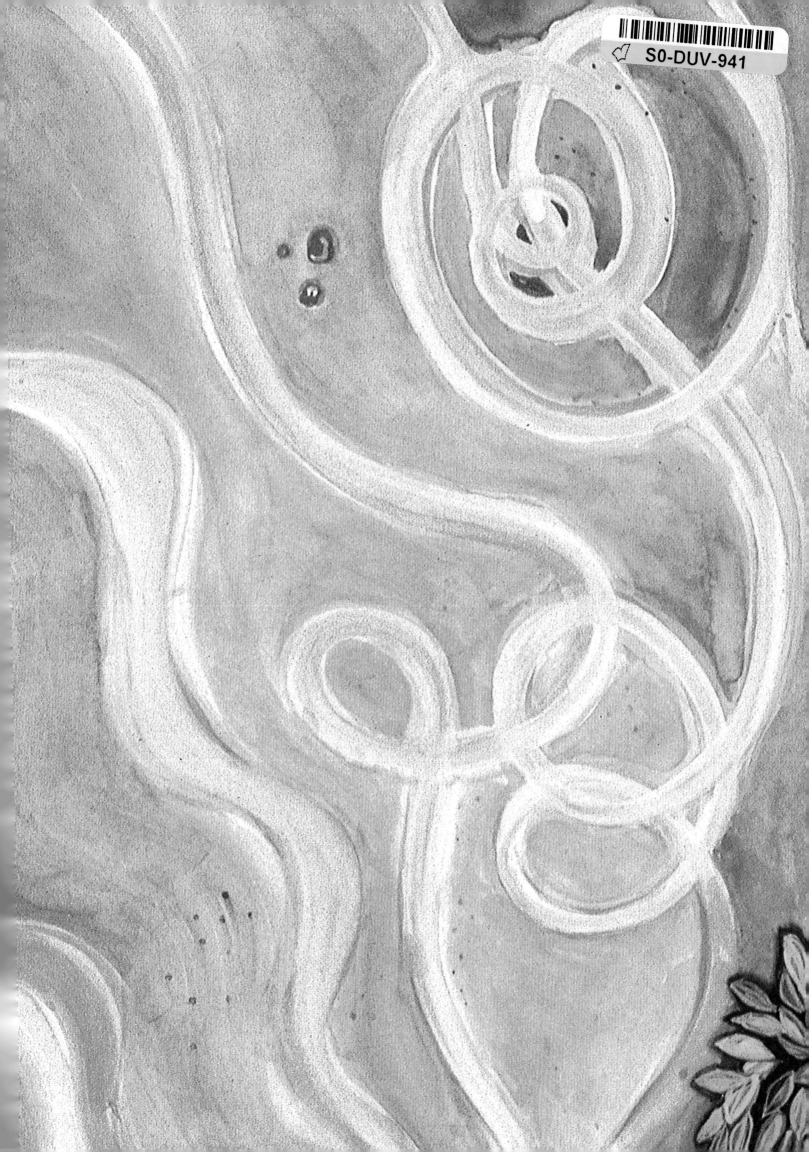

Snakey Jake to the Rescue!

Story by Roxanne Capaul
Illustrations by Anne Whiting

Published by Rotire, Inc.

Story and Editorial Directon by Roxanne Capaul
Production Artist / Bob Schram

Snakey Jake™ to the Rescue / Paintings by Anne Whiting
The Paintings in this book are watercolor / mixed media on paper

ISBN 0-9719222-0-9
Published by Rotire, Inc.

Printed in Korea by Asianprinting.com

In Memory of
Woody, my Best Friend

For all of the wonderful and
crazy ways that you brought joy
into my life.
And for going on with courage
against great odds … You are
my Hero.

S nakey Jake lives in the forest, not far from the Blue Lake, near the Brown Mountains in Brisbie County. There are many large snake families living there, and Snakey Jake knows them all. He visits his snake friends almost every day. They laugh and play silly snake games and make funny designs in the sand with their long tails.

ne morning, Snakey Jake went to visit his new neighbors a short distance away. A Family of raccoons had just moved in. Mother and father raccoon were hard at work making their home warm and cozy.

They didn't notice Snakey Jake approaching through the tall grass and were surprised to see him watching them as they did their chores. At first the raccoons were afraid when they saw Snakey Jake. After all, he was a snake and a strange looking one at that. Snakey Jake just kept coming, smiling his sweet snake smile.

"Good morning!" he said. "My name is Snakey Jake. You have a nice family. I have a wonderful family too. Would you like to come to my home for dinner?"

The raccoon family stared at the big snake. He seemed friendly. All of the scary stories they had heard about snakes made them leery of his offer. But the mother raccoon saw something special about Snakey Jake that made her trust him.

With a warm smile, she replied "I think that would be fun. We are new here and look forward to making friends. Please tell your mother we will come tomorrow night if that would be all right?" Snakey Jake was so excited, "Oh yes, I will tell her right away!"

As soon as Snakey Jake had disappeared into the woods, father raccoon spoke to his wife. "Are you sure you want to visit a family of snakes? Remember the stories we heard about snakes hurting small animals?" "That's true" she said, "but there have been stories about raccoons that were not true. I really think we can trust Snakey Jake."

Snakey Jake couldn't wait to tell his family. His mother was cleaning the den when he told her the news. "Mother, I met a nice raccoon family and invited them to dinner tomorrow night!" His mother looked at him with a twinkle in her eye. That was just like Snakey Jake, making friends with everyone. She was surprised to hear that raccoons would spend the evening with snakes. After all, you know the stories! But she was delighted and began to prepare for the following night.

That night while Snakey Jake and his brothers and sisters were playing in the sand, something strange happened.

Suddenly, they all stopped and stared at Snakey Jake. "What?" he asked. His tail glowed with an orangish yellow light. They all gathered around, worried there was something wrong with him. But Snakey Jake liked the bright tail. It made it easier to see the designs in the sand now that the sun had gone down.

Soon their mother came looking for them. To her surprise they were all playing in a halo of bright light that seemed to come from Snakey Jake's tail!

"Oh my!" she exclaimed. "It's ok mother," said the smallest snake. "Snakey Jake is all right, he just has" … right at that moment the light went out. Then suddenly it came back on. Laughing, Snakey Jake said, "I think I can turn it on and off!" They all watched as his tail began to blink. It was amazing!

eanwhile the raccoon family was busy meeting other neighbors and talking about their dinner plans with the snake family. They were all very nervous and afraid about the raccoons spending the evening with snakes. After all, the stories you know! Mother raccoon assured them that she felt safe visiting Snakey Jake's family. She told them about the gentle snake that had come to visit, and how she knew she could trust him.

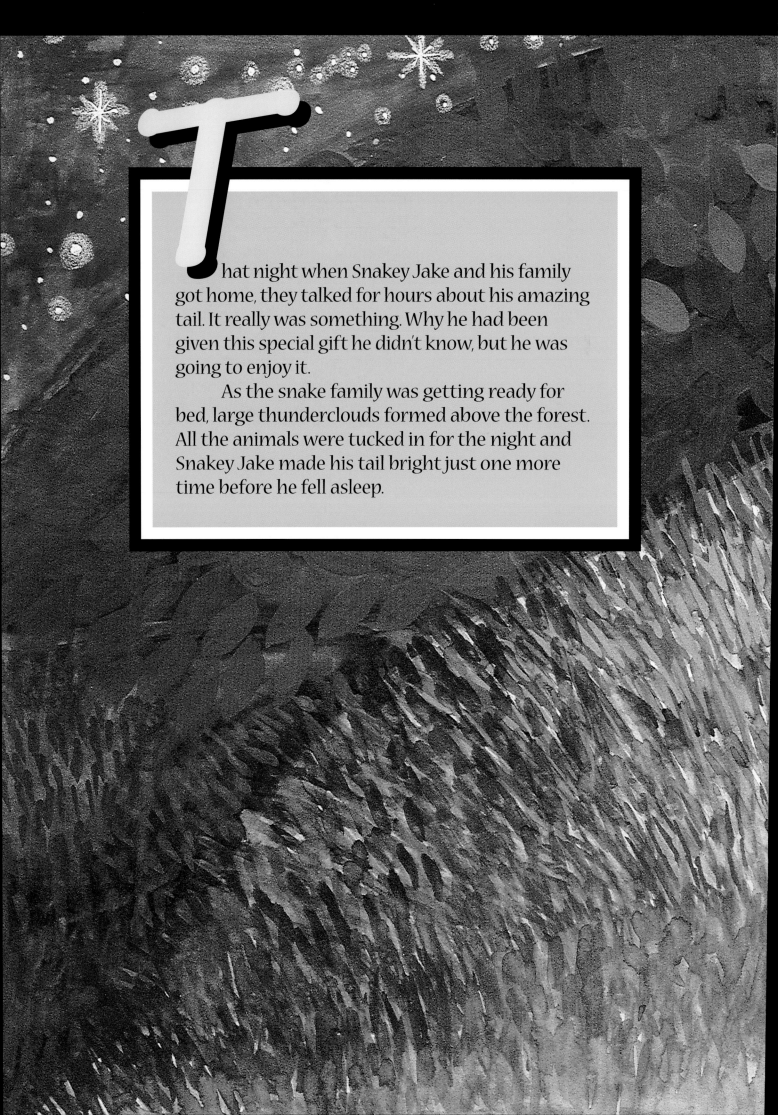

That night when Snakey Jake and his family got home, they talked for hours about his amazing tail. It really was something. Why he had been given this special gift he didn't know, but he was going to enjoy it.

As the snake family was getting ready for bed, large thunderclouds formed above the forest. All the animals were tucked in for the night and Snakey Jake made his tail bright just one more time before he fell asleep.

Early the next morning, a loud boom of thunder woke every creature in the forest. The rain started to pour from the sky.

Snakey Jake and his family spent the day making plans for the dinner party. By early evening, the thunder and lightning had almost stopped, but the rain still came down in sheets, making the forest wet and slippery.

The animals in the forest were used to the rainy weather so the raccoon family decided to bundle up and make the short trip through the woods to Snakey Jake's home.

nakey Jake could see the raccoons making their way to the den and the sight of the babies rolling and sliding in the mud was comical. They were having fun, and barely resembled the cute little raccoons he had met the day before.

Snakey Jake yelled to his family to come and greet their guests. The snake family was startled at the sight before them. All at once, everyone started laughing and Snakey Jake knew the evening would be a success.

Because of the weather, the parents wanted the children to play inside. Snakey Jake and his brothers and sisters had made lots of tunnels in and out of the many dens, so they decided to give the raccoon babies a tour of their favorite tunnel, which was long and twisting and lead to the Blue Lake.

When they reached the opening at the end of the tunnel, Snakey Jake suddenly said, "Shhh … everyone be quiet!" In the distance he could hear the faint cries of a mother duck. Snakey Jake knew the sound of someone in trouble. He said, "Something's wrong, I'm going to go and see, but I want you all to go back to the den and wait for me with our parents."

The smallest snake didn't want him to go. Snakey Jake assured him that it would be ok and he slithered off into the dark and stormy night.

The baby raccoons and the little snakes rushed back to their parents. Soon worried faces filled the den. Snakey Jake's mother asked, "Where is Snakey Jake?"

The smallest snake explained that Snakey Jake had gone to see what the trouble was out by the Blue Lake. The look on the faces of Snakey Jake's parents was mournful. There was such a storm and it was cold and dark outside. They all decided to go to the end of the tunnel and look for some sign of Snakey Jake.

Snakey Jake was worried too. He knew that the mother duck was afraid of snakes. But he had to see if he could help. The sounds were getting louder, and as he entered a small opening in the brush, he saw what was happening.

The mother duck stood on the shore frantically crying to her small ducklings to step accross a floating log to get back to land. But the babies were terrified. The water was churning and the rain was so heavy that they couldn't see to jump. They would surely drown if they stayed where they were much longer.

Snakey Jake had never been in the water and was not sure he could swim. But he had to save the babies. As he slithered into the water, he concentrated on lighting his tail so the ducklings could see the log and find their way. As the mother duck stood feeling helpless, Snakey Jake swam across the lake. The mother duck saw the movement in the water and the bright light that followed it. Was it some horrible creature coming to get her babies?

All she could do was quack a loud warning to her babies. As Snakey Jake got closer, he saw that the log had moved too far away. So he swam as close as possible and tried to convince them to jump onto his back and he would carry them to the shore.

The ducklings were scared enough already and now there was a snake with a light on his tail telling them to jump on his back! They looked for their mother, but the rain made it impossible to see her. Snakey Jake said, "I know you are really scared, so am I, but you have to trust me. Please climb onto my back. The light will show us the way."

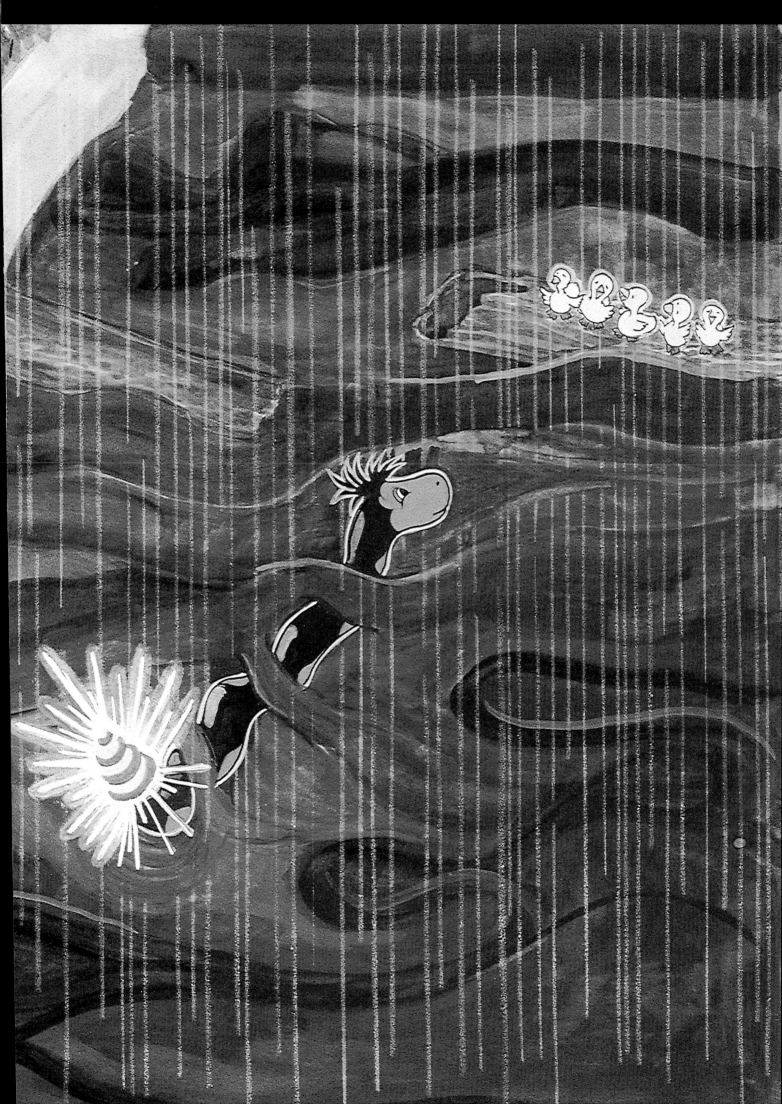

The first little duckling liked the big snake's voice and decided he could trust him. When he jumped onto his back, the others followed. They clung on for dear life all the way to the shore where their mother anxiously waited. Snakey Jake carefully slithered onto the land and one by one they jumped off of his back and scurried to their mother. When he knew they were all safe, Snakey Jake quietly slipped away into the night. The mother duck turned to thank the great snake that had saved her babies, but all she saw was a soft orangish yellow glow fading off into the distance.

It took Snakey Jake a long time to make his way back to the den. His family could see a beam of light coming through the woods.

They waited anxiously. Finally he appeared through the rain and they all rushed to him with hugs and kisses. Even the baby raccoons tried hard to get their little arms around the big snake.

The rest of the evening they talked about the rescue. Snakey Jake was very tired and happy when he could finally go to bed and get a good nights sleep.

The next morning the snake family was up early. All except Snakey Jake. He was going to sleep in. It was a well deserved rest.

There was a gathering of animals in the forest. The raccoon family had spread the word about the rescue the night before and how the big snake with the bright tail had saved the baby ducklings. They all wanted to do something special for Snakey Jake. They soon came up with an idea.

Snakey Jake woke up to bright sunshine and the wonderful smell of breakfast. He made his way to the family den, where everyone was gathered and waiting for the hero. He didn't feel special. He just did what he had to do.

The storm had passed and it would be nice to bask in the sun and think about the days ahead and all of the new adventures with his friends the raccoons. Friends were so important to Snakey Jake. It made him happy just to think about it.

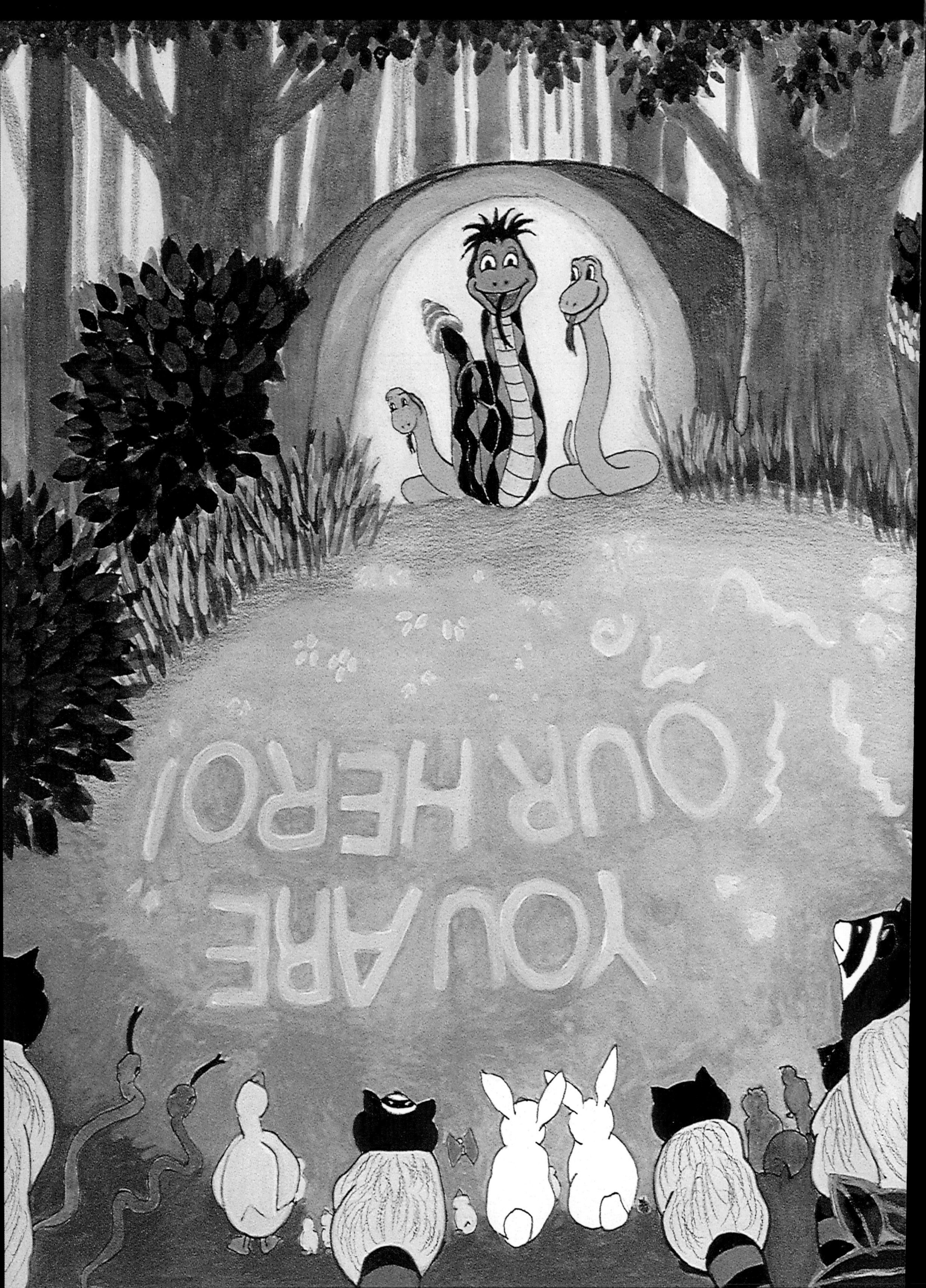
YOU ARE
OUR HERO!

The creatures in the forest had thought about how to thank Snakey Jake for coming to the rescue. They knew that all he really wanted was to have friends and be happy. They all came to the entrance of the den and made a message in the sand for the wonderful snake. It read: YOU ARE OUR HERO!

All of the animals big and small signed their names in the sand with swirls and curls, it made a beautiful design.

Snakey Jake and his family heard the excitement outside and hurried to see what was happening. When Snakey Jake saw the message and all of the animals standing in a circle, he was so happy, his tail lit up like the sun. It was brighter than ever.

The forest was forever changed by the friend-ships that came about that day. All those stories about snakes seemed to disappear. And if you look very closely on a dark night … you can see a glow coming from the forest by the Blue Lake next to the Brown Mountains in Brisbie County.